DRAGONS IN SPACE

DRAGONS IN SPACE

DRAGON APPROVED™ BOOK TEN

RAMY VANCE

MICHAEL ANDERLE

THE DRAGONS IN SPACE TEAM

Thanks to the JIT Readers

Kathleen Fettig
Diane L. Smith
Kelly O'Donnell
Dave Hicks
Deb Mader
John Ashmore
Veronica Stephan-Miller
Dorothy Lloyd
Kerry Mortimer

If we've missed anyone, please let us know!

Editor
The Skyhunter Editing Team

Copyright © 2020 by Ramy Vance & Michael Anderle
Cover Art by Jake @ J Caleb Design
http://jcalebdesign.com / jcalebdesign@gmail.com
Cover copyright © LMBPN Publishing
A Michael Anderle Production

LMBPN Publishing
PMB 196, 2540 South Maryland Pkwy
Las Vegas, NV 89109

First US Edition, May 2020
eBook ISBN: 978-1-64202-911-6
Print ISBN: 978-1-64202-912-3

DEDICATION

Dedicated to the NHS workers who are navigating this crisis with grace and dignity..

—Ramy

*To Family, Friends and
Those Who Love
to Read.
May We All Enjoy Grace
to Live the Life We Are
Called.*

— Michael

CHAPTER ONE

The skies of Earth have an understated beauty. It's as if when they took form, they wished to be seen as ordinary. They are the sort of skies that open up to you. They are human skies.

In the nine realms, there are skies that are filled with stars throughout the day and the night, skies that boast two suns or three moons, and skies that hold hosts of floating whales and creatures made from the stuff of myths. Yet whenever an elf or gnome steps onto Earth for the first time and is greeted with the accepting blue skies peppered with clouds that look soft enough to sleep on, they stop and stare. There is a beauty in the simplicity of Earth's sky, one that cannot be easily understood or replicated.

It was this sky that Alex and the rest of Team Boundless tore into. A portal with a two-mile radius opened over the Big Sky state of Montana.

The portal was from the hadron collider at the Wasps Nest, one of the older models. It was Myrddin's first attempt to find a way for humans to move throughout the realms without spells cast by magi or the use of a familiar. This collider wasn't as precise as the newer models, and it tended to make oversized portals that could easily be noticed by many different kinds of technology.

A metallic warship roughly the size of a Navy aircraft carrier floated out of the portal. It buckled for a moment before it adjusted to the gravity of the planet, firing its thrusters to even out and remain in the air.

The ship was running a skeleton crew, just enough to keep it operational. Myrddin didn't have enough recruits or officers to spare, so they were making do with what was available. The crew was in the main viewing area of the craft.

And because most of them had never been to Earth before, all duties were put on hold as they crowded around the windows.

Manny, a Beholder who headed up the recruitment process for the dragonriders and just about any other group that had to deal with the human realm, was one of the few passengers who didn't seem interested in the view. Instead, his many eyes were poring over a collection of paper and digital dossiers.

The other person seemingly uninterested in the ship's descent through Earth's skies was Alex, the leader of Team Boundless. As the rest of her team clambered to the viewing ports, Alex sat near Manny, reading a book on the theories behind human integration of draconic fluids. She yawned loudly as she read. The book was far from interesting.

Manny looked up from his work, one of his eyes narrowing as he watched Alex reading. "Would've thought you'd be more interested in being home," Manny murmured under his breath but loud enough for Alex to hear, then even louder, "Some people would kill for this kind of shore leave."

She tried to ignore Manny, concentrating on her book's text. It was difficult. She was having a hard enough time paying attention to what she was reading, but it was better than trying to crowd around with everyone and pretend to be excited.

Manny was right; most people *would* have been excited about the chance to go home. Alex wasn't one of them, though. Nervous wasn't the word. She was more stressed than she'd ever been, and that was saying a lot since her life had devolved into a series of tense battles and events.

Alex looked down at her robotic hand. She'd left in such a rush, she hadn't been able to head to the med bay and see if they had anything to make her arm any less noticeable. She wasn't looking forward to explaining how she had lost her arm to her parents.

There was going to be a lot of yelling and crying, and that wasn't the way to spend her first day home.

Alex glanced at the rest of the crew, who were losing their minds over the Montana skies. She was glad they were all enjoying themselves. She had even heard Brath, the perpetually grouchy gnome who seemed to despise human culture, gasp in awe when the ship had exited the collider portal.

It was probably better to give the team some space and let them take everything in on their own without risking raining on their parade. That was all she was able to do. There was too much on her mind to be social right now. Thoughts ran through her head faster than her dragon Chine could fly.

Before Alex left the Nest, she had spoken with Myrddin about the alien Vardis, who had come to Middang3ard with the promise of a weapon that could destroy the Dark One. From the get-go, Myrddin didn't seem to want Vardis' help.

The wizard had disclosed his fears to Alex before she and the team had left. He didn't trust the alien. There were many different factors going into Myrddin's opinion, and he didn't know where he stood on the situation. It was an odd thing for a wizard who had been managing the war efforts for so long to be so indecisive.

Alex still didn't know what she thought of the situation. On the one hand, it would make sense for Myrddin to be mistrustful of an unknown variable such as Vardis. The wizard knew what was going on in the nine realms, and anything outside his sphere of influence would seem untrustworthy.

On the other hand, he had brought up a couple of points that had embarrassed Alex but that she couldn't disagree with. Vardis would only speak with Alex. At first, she had taken it as an insult that Myrddin thought this was a reason to be suspicious.

Alex had led three missions against all odds and had come out alive. She was steadily growing a reputation in the Nest as one of the best dragonriders in the Corps. That was what made Myrddin's words so hard to swallow, but he was right.

Alex was only a kid, one who was still piecing together what was going on in the war and who didn't have nearly as good an understanding of the war effort as Myrddin. If Vardis talked to anyone, it should have been Myrddin. Alex could see that now.

Needless to say, all this made going home for a dinner with her family more than a little troubling.

Manny cleared his throat loudly, catching Alex's attention. "Are you planning on ignoring me for this entire ride? I haven't seen you in weeks, and then it was hardly any more than a curt hello. You humans never cease to puzzle me."

Alex sighed as she closed her book and placed it on the table next to her. "Sorry, Manny, I just have a lot on my mind. And you seem to be very busy."

"Part of my job is looking out for your well-being when I'm around, and you don't look like you're doing very well, if I may say. All that stuff on your mind dragging you down?"

"It's just…well, how much do you trust Myrddin?"

Manny put down his dossier, all of his eyes focusing on Alex. "What do you mean?"

Alex threw her hands up. "Not like that. I know he's trustworthy. I just mean, do you think he's always right? Do you ever doubt him?"

"Rarely," the Beholder said, "but sometimes, yes. He's not infallible. He's human. An old human but a human nonetheless."

"When was the last time you thought he was making a mistake?"

Manny smiled as he turned back to his work. "When he suggested recruiting a blind human to be a dragonrider. We both saw how that turned out, didn't we?"

Alex slouched back in her chair and groaned. "Manny, I'm not trying to fish for reassurance, I'm being serious."

Manny didn't bother looking up from his work this time. "I am being serious. Humans are notorious for not having quick enough reflexes to be dragonriders. It's the whole reason we have mech riders. And from what I understood of humans, being able to see was pretty important to riding. On paper, it all looked like a terrible idea. Yet here we are."

Alex felt like Manny was trying to guilt her into blindly accepting Myrddin's wisdom. True, she hadn't seen any reason not to, but it still seemed like a bad idea to blindly follow anyone. "I'm not saying I don't appreciate what—"

Manny interrupted. "Neither am I. Just saying I have my doubts too. I usually hope Myrddin is right."

Alex wished Manny had heard what the wizard had told her about Vardis. There was nothing Alex wanted more than for Myrddin to be wrong about that one. She hoped this was as straightforward as Vardis having a weapon that worked. Then they could put an end to this damn war.

Jollies, a pixie with skin that flashed different colors

depending on her mood, flew over to Alex. The pixie was about as long as Alex's hand and often stood on her palm to talk. This time she zipped over and landed on the human's shoulder. "You never told me Earth was so beautiful."

Alex sighed and stood up. She wasn't going to be able to sit this one out. Her roommate had come over to talk to her, so she either couldn't take a hint or didn't care. "Okay, okay, I'll come check out the view with you."

Most of Team Boundless were gathered at the same viewing portal. They were passengers on this one, though, their dragons traveling on a separate carrier heading toward an Earth base with an appropriate setup.

Alex squeezed in next to Jim, another human who was part of their team. Jim wasn't a dragonrider but was one of the mech riders, a group of humans and elves who piloted dragon mechs.

As she took her spot, Jim reached down and quickly squeezed her hand. "How does it feel to be back home?"

Alex forced a smile as she avoided his eyes, looking out the viewing window and watching the clouds roll by. "Good," she lied. "I can hardly believe I'm back here. Visiting has been all I've been able to think about."

Jim watched Alex closely as if he wasn't sure what to make of her words. "Yeah, same here, I guess," he finally replied. "It's going to be great to see my folks. Still can't believe we're here. Honestly, I forgot Earth existed for a little while. This is a good reminder."

Next to Jim stood Brath, the red-headed gnome. Alex didn't ever miss a chance to give him a hard time, and now was as good a time as any. Brath seemed to be genuinely in awe of the sky. "Hey, Brath, you gonna pick your jaw up off the ground anytime soon?" she quipped.

Brath slowly turned his head until he was facing Alex, his

eyes still wide and a little dreamy. "Wait, what? Did you say something?"

"You okay, dude?"

"Yeah, definitely, definitely," he murmured as he turned back to the view.

Gill, who was standing beside Brath, leaned behind the gnome and tapped Jim on the shoulder, hissing a little to catch Alex's attention as well. "Brath is from a community of deep gnomes," Gill explained. "They rarely see the sky when they're growing up. As a result, the first time deep gnomes see a new sky, they go into something like a trance. It's similar to a recreational drug. He'll probably do the same when he sees the sunset here, too."

Brath punched Gill in the kneecap. "What have I told you about babbling on about why I do what I do?"

Gill laughed and shoved Brath playfully. "I only wanted to let the humans know why you're behaving so adorably. Didn't want them to think you were getting soft."

"I'm not getting soft. It's just so damn beautiful," Brath murmured.

The rest of them couldn't help but laugh at Brath's attitude change. The gnome didn't seem to mind. He was thoroughly engrossed in the sky.

A voice came through the intercom. "Please return to your seats. We're going to begin our descent. We should be on the ground in ten minutes."

The team grumbled as they complied, but Alex couldn't have been happier. Staring out the window had been making her anxious. She would have preferred to have been riding Chine. Instead, she was locked up on a ship, trying to pretend her mind wasn't racing a mile a minute.

She took a seat across from Manny. "Are you coming with us?"

Manny shook his head as he leafed through papers.

"Nope, not this time. Just here to get you to the base. After that, it's just you, the team, and Vardis."

"What do you mean, Vardis?"

"Myrddin didn't tell you? Vardis is going with you guys. Guess he thought it would be better for you to keep an eye on him."

"Than for him to remain in quarantine?"

Manny rolled some of his eyes as he continued to read. "Like I said, sometimes I have my doubts. Things usually work out, though."

Alex hoped the Beholder was right.

CHAPTER TWO

The carrier touched down on a base on the plains, far from any form of civilization. From the sky, it looked like a blip in the wilderness.

Once the carrier had landed, the doors opened and the main crew filed out, leaving only the dragonriders and Manny. That was when Alex realized she had no idea what was supposed to be happening other than arriving on Earth. Now she realized why Manny had been sent along. Myrddin must have thought it would be easier to send a chaperone than to explain all the details.

Just as Alex had suspected, Manny was gathering his things. He transported them into a void realm, then approached Team Boundless. "Looks like it's time to get going," the Beholder said as he floated past the teenagers, who exchanged glances for a moment before following him. No one except Alex was used to taking orders from Manny.

Outside the carrier, the crew had lined up and were being talked to by the commander of the base they had just arrived at. Manny led the dragonriders into the base, which looked worlds different than the Wasps Nest.

Alex had never seen a military base before—truthfully, the Nest was the first base of any kind she'd ever *seen*—but the Nest and this base were two very different places.

What Alex first noticed was the difference in the air. There was something about the air at the Nest. Alex had thought it was unnamable while she was there, but now she knew what the scent was: it was magic.

The air at this base, however, was as unmagical as it got. It smelled like oil and old grease and sweat. Like a place where a lot of people worked very hard.

Another difference was the lack of advanced tech. Manny had to open a door with his eye tentacles, a feat that took a few minutes despite Alex and Jim offering to help.

Once the riders were inside, Alex marveled at the sheer size of the base. Its construction was impressive in the simple way that all human things seemed to be. The base reminded Alex of photos her dad had sent her of his office since she'd gotten her vision.

The rest of the team didn't seem to be the least bit disappointed. Jollies and Brath stared fixedly at everything the team walked past as they followed Manny down the halls. The vending machines interested Brath the most. He couldn't understand why humans would be so cruel as to put food behind a glass wall.

Jollies was mystified by how dark it was. Alex wouldn't have noticed if Jollies hadn't brought it up, but the pixie was right. Not that the base was badly lit; it was just a different kind of lighting than she was used to. The Nest probably didn't use electricity for power.

Manny continued to lead the riders through the halls as they talked. Brath and Jollies were full of questions about how humans could create such a depressing-looking place, and whether Alex had seen anything like this before. The two were very disappointed when Alex reminded them she had been blind for her whole life. She hadn't seen a lot of things. Still, they pestered her with questions until she finally groaned and told them to ask Jim, whose father was in the military. If anyone could answer their questions, it was Jim.

Jollies and Brath wasted no time accosting Jaws with their questions, and he did everything he could to answer them. Gill, as usual, was quiet, watching and listening to what others were saying, his eyes soft and deep in thought. Alex wondered what the drow was thinking about all this.

Finally, they rounded a corner and came to the only part of the base that looked remotely familiar: the quarantine area. It seemed that Myrddin had done some upgrading to help the human base house Vardis, who sat in a glass-walled room. He stood when he saw the riders walking toward him. "Greetings, Manny, riders," he said politely.

One of Manny's eyes stared at Alex. Without eyebrows or a face to go along with the eye, it was always difficult to figure out what Manny was trying to convey. "Good to see you as well," he said as the door opened.

The alien stepped out of the room. He was a couple of inches taller than the dragonriders. "How was your ride over?"

"Teleporting on an air carrier is preferable to any other method of transport. At least I had a bathroom to throw up in."

Vardis nodded as if he understood. "Once the Dark One is defeated, my people will have much technology to share with yours. There is no doubt it will usher in a grand age for your people. It is not uncommon for a civilization to be propelled forward because of alien technology."

Alex chuckled to herself. It sounded like Vardis had been reading alien conspiracy books like her dad. From everything she'd seen so far, none of the other races of the nine realms needed help jumping forward. And almost all of the tech at the Nest had been created by humans under Myrddin's supervision.

It seemed odd to Alex. Vardis still hadn't told any of them what the weapon was. Even if Alex had trusted Vardis originally, Myrddin had laid seeds of doubt in her mind. It was going to be hard not to see everything Vardis did or said through that lens, but was that any way to work with him?

The Beholder and the alien broke away from everyone else and started to talk. Alex thought that was strange. There was no reason to assume Vardis had information for Manny, given the way he'd acted before. Many things seemed questionable now that suspicion had been introduced to her mind.

Team Boundless stood around like a bunch of children. That infuriated Alex, but there was nothing she could do about it. She wasn't certain what they were here for besides the weapon on the moon, which she was going to be responsible for acquiring.

Manny floated away from Vardis and over to Alex. He looked uncertain. "So," he began, "your parents asked if you'd be able to have dinner with them tonight. We were wondering if you'd be comfortable bringing the team with you."

Alex grinned widely. Uncertain as she was about the whole situation, she'd been looking forward to her parents meeting her friends, even if it might make her parents uncomfortable. "Of course!"

"And we were also wondering if you'd be comfortable bringing Vardis along."

The question made a lump form in Alex's throat. She tried to answer, but nothing came out. Luckily, Manny didn't push it. "Of course, you'll have time to think that over. It is a bit much to ask you to spring gnomes, pixies, elves, *and* aliens on your parents in one sitting."

Alex quickly recovered, making it seem as if she hadn't been bothered by the question at all. "Yeah, it would be a lot to drop on them," she answered. "When would that be?"

"After we take care of some necessities. We still need to get your dragons outfitted for the mission. Since we're running on a pretty tight schedule, I figured it would be better to prep the dragons before the final touches are put on. Follow me."

Manny floated away. Team Boundless followed him as he led them yet through another lengthy set of winding hallways. The farther they went into the military base, the more it reminded Alex of the Nest. Even the smell of magic was present.

The dragons were housed in a smaller version of the stables from the Nest. Alex recognized the design as soon as she walked into the room. Granted, it wasn't nearly as large or open, but whoever had constructed it had put in a lot of work to make sure the dragons had enough space.

It looked as if the room could easily accommodate at least fifteen dragons, but it didn't seem to be in use yet.

Alex walked farther into the makeshift stables, happy to come across something that felt familiar. She reached out to Chine telepathically. His response was nearly instantaneous. *Finally! I thought you were never going to get here.*

CHAPTER THREE

All of the dragonriders' dragons were currently housed in the makeshift stables. The riders were ecstatic to see their dragons again. Alex was surprised by how happy she was to hear Chine's voice in her head. It hadn't been that long since she had last seen him.

Alex leaped into Chine's nest, threw her arms around his neck, and said hello. Chine seemed just as happy to see her. *So, this is Earth? I didn't think I would live long enough to see this place.*

Death? Alex had never heard Chine mention his mortality. It caught her off-guard. *What do you mean, live long enough to see Earth?* she asked.

Chine stretched out his wings as he peeked over the edge of his nest, checking on what the rest of the riders and dragons were up to. *Dragons live for a very long time, but I am very aware that my life might not reach its natural length due to our situation.*

What's our situation?

The war. The constant battles.

Alex was glad she'd caught herself before she snapped at

him. For some reason, she had thought Chine was implying that his death was part of their bonding.

The idea was so foreign that Alex could have sworn it came from someone else. It was the opposite of what she'd been feeling about the dragon only a few seconds ago. Hopefully, he didn't notice. She would keep it to herself. *Do you think they're going to let us take you to meet with my parents?*

Chine shook his head and chuckled. *I doubt it. Where would we stay while you eat? Besides, I would prefer to have my augments installed over the night as well. These are supposed to be easier to deal with than the ones in Middang3ard. I'd like to see if that is true.*

Alex stayed with him for a bit longer, the two of them talking in the fashion that they had both grown comfortable with. The thought didn't often cross Alex's mind, but she was suddenly reminded of how much she appreciated the dragon being in her life.

The ether dragon was the being she was closest to in the whole world. Even when they weren't talking to each other, they were in contact. Thoughts and feelings passed between the two of them on such an instinctual level that Alex never thought twice about it.

That was what was happening at the moment. Neither Chine nor Alex was purposely sending anything, but they were still playing off each other's thoughts, letting them wash through and responding in kind. It was a different kind of interchange than Alex had experienced with any of the other telepaths in Middang3ard.

Telepathy reminded her of Vardis. The two of them were linked now. Was that a good idea? Especially since she was linked to Chine too. Did that mean that Vardis had access to the dragon's mind?

Reassurance from Chine poured over Alex like warm

15

water. *No, he doesn't have access to my mind. I am a stronger telepath than most, stronger than the alien.*

Do you think it's okay to trust him? I mean, he's coming to dinner with us all from what Manny told me.

Chine folded his claws over each other and rested his head on them as he stared at Alex with his deep-black eyes. *Trust is a difficult thing to understand. On the one hand, we have no reason to believe anything this Vardis says. And on the other, how are we to defeat the Dark One without trusting those who share in our fight?*

The dragon had a point. The other races of the nine realms had to have learned to trust each other over the years they'd worked together. Just because they were getting along now didn't mean things had always been like that. There had to have been a period of time during which they were all building that trust. *I guess bringing him to dinner is a pretty good first step.*

I would think so.

Alex looked down at her dragon anchor to check the time. *I should get going. I'm pretty sure I have to do a briefing with Manny before we're allowed to leave the base. I'll see you in a bit, big guy.*

Alex prepared to leave and suddenly stopped. *Hey, I just thought of something. When I'm not around, what do you do?*

Chine stood up on his hind legs and leaned over the edge of the nest as Alex climbed out. *Usually, we're left to our own devices. I have friends, much like you. Since none of us are near our families, those in the Nest have become our family. Generally, we're allowed to come and go as we please. Unfortunately, that will not be the case during our time on Earth.*

I'm really sorry you have to be cooped up the whole time we're here.

Chine winked at Alex and then exhaled a small cloud of dust, the dragon equivalent of shrugging. *Nothing to worry about. I have my friends. Timber and I have plans to teach Furi meditation techniques. He could use some calm.*

Alex laughed as she turned to leave and find Manny. *"Him and Brath both,"* she said over her shoulder.

Alex found the Beholder in the mess hall, staring at a bowl of sad-looking soup. He seemed to be in the same state as the soup. Most of his eyes looked up when he saw Alex. "You know, when I found out I was coming to Earth, I had my hopes set pretty high," he said. "This is only the first stop, and I'm praying this doesn't set the bar for the whole trip."

Alex took a seat across from Manny and peered at his soup. It looked like brown sludge with bits of vegetables floating on the surface. "My dad's cooking is much better than that."

"That won't help me. I'm not joining you for dinner, just Boundless and Vardis. Your family is going to be the ambassadors for all things human."

Alex gulped. *All things human? Sure, why not add a little more pressure,* she thought. "Why aren't you coming? Don't you want to keep an eye on everything?"

Manny poked his soup as if he thought that would make it more appealing. "No, I trust you, and so does Myrddin."

Alex considered his words and nodded slowly. "This is a very different trip than the last few."

"Think of it as a short vacation. Nothing's trying to kill you. We're just picking up something hidden in one of the safest quadrants of the nine realms. It's about time we all got a break."

As Manny started to slurp his soup, Vardis walked into the mess hall. He took his time walking over to the table, and he stood awkwardly once he arrived. "Are you going to sit down?" Alex asked, slightly annoyed by how uncomfortable the alien seemed.

Vardis looked confused by the question. "Is that the most appropriate way to handle these kinds of situations?"

Alex scooted over to make room for him. "Yeah, definitely," she explained. "When we go to my parents' house, we'll be sitting and talking. If you see a bunch of people sitting, it's usually a good idea to sit as well. Otherwise, people think you're trying to rush them."

Vardis seemed to be paying attention, but it was hard to tell with his dark eyes. "Excited to meet my family?" she continued to make conversation. She hadn't talked to the alien about anything other than the weapon yet.

Manny continued eating, probably happy to not be included in the conversation.

Vardis watched the Beholder slurping his food. "Yes, this will be my first meal with humans. I am very excited to partake. And then we will retrieve the weapon from your moon, correct?"

"Yep, that's the whole reason we're here. That and to give everyone an idea about how great Earth is. Maybe they'll fight even harder to keep this place from blowing up."

"The Dark One does not blow planets up. He eats them from the inside until there is nothing left and they collapse in on themselves, killing everyone who was sustained by their place of birth."

Alex and Manny exchanged glances in the dead quiet that followed his statement. "Uh, it was just a phrase," the rider murmured. "Try not to say that at dinner if you can help it."

Vardis blinked in surprise, looking like a giant insect. "Say what?"

"Never mind. I take it back. Just be yourself. Let's hope it works out."

It didn't take long for Team Boundless to be ready to leave. Alex explained to her team that they didn't have to adhere to any specific customs for the visit. That was a relief for everyone involved, but despite Alex's constant reassurances, Jollies, Brath, and Gill wore their best formal clothes to meet Alex's parents.

Gill's formal drow suit was far too proper for a small get-together of friends. The suit was hand-stitched by one of the finest tailors in Gill's community. Each thread could be seen individually and glimmered like a polished jewel. The narrow outline of the suit gave way to a flowing robe past the waist. It was a very flattering outfit.

Brath, on the other hand, had chosen a rough suit of dwarfish chainmail armor. He explained that it was mostly ceremonial. His father had passed it on to him, and his father before him. It had never seen battle, which was good since the armor was old enough to fall apart under the weakest of plasma blasts.

Jollies hadn't worn anything special but whispered to Alex that pixies as well as fairies attended all major social events in the nude. She had thought it better to ask Alex ahead of time and joked, "It's not hard to dress down."

Once everyone had changed into something more comfortable, Boundless headed out to meet Alex's parents.

For the first time in months, Alex stood at her front door. The last time she'd been here was when Manny and Myrddin had come to recruit her. Now she was about to knock with a host of other races in tow. Hopefully, her parents wouldn't freak out too much.

The door was opened almost instantly. Her mother and father crowded the threshold. Liza and George were all smiles, both of them trying to blink back tears. George leaned forward, scooped Alex up in his arms, and squeezed her tightly. "It's so good to finally see you again, kiddo." He laughed as he tightened his grip.

Alex managed a weak hello with the little bit of air she had in her lungs before her father dropped her. She gave her mom a kiss, and Liza promptly burst into tears and rushed to wipe them away.

George stepped back, motioning for the rest of the guests to come in. "Please, don't stand outside. It's time we got to know each other."

Alex walked into the house, surprised her parents weren't caught off guard by a gnome, a dark elf, and a pixie. Why her parents didn't notice the alien standing at the rear was beyond Alex's understanding. Even Jim seemed to think it was weird. He leaned over and said, "My parents would be losing their minds right now."

George and Liza stood in the living room as the rest of the group awkwardly glanced at Alex, waiting for her to take the lead on the introductions.

After the introductions were over, she asked, "So, you guys aren't weirded out by this?"

Liza laughed as she waved away Alex's question. "Of course not, honey. After you left, your dad and I decided we had to check out *Middang3ard* VR. It didn't make sense to be completely in the dark about what you were getting involved in. We each got our own set. Spending date nights in *Middang3ard* has made them a lot more interesting."

George took a seat in his recliner. "Not to toot our own horns too loudly, but we've become kind of a big deal in there," he said lazily, trying to downplay how happy he was with himself.

Jollies flitted over to Alex's shoulder and whispered, "Your parents seem really cool."

Alex wasn't expecting that to be her friends' reaction. "Wait until they talk more."

George, who hadn't heard Alex, leaned forward in his chair and said, "You might have heard of us. KillerStud313 and HotMammaBlood."

Jollies' skin shifted from its formerly calming blue to bright, excited pink. "Wait! That's you guys? Oh, my gods! You guys are legends!"

Alex couldn't believe what she was hearing come out of Jollies' mouth. "Are you serious?"

Jollies flew in front of Alex's face and grabbed her by the cheeks. "These two single-handedly beat the end-game raid that takes eighteen people to finish! The only party to ever finish it faster was the Mundanes, and we all know how good they are."

Alex stared at her parents. Liza didn't seem to think it was a big deal, but George was smiling smugly, obviously proud of himself. "Well, I mean, we hold other records," he said as well. "But we can talk about that over dinner. Now, which of you is giving me a hand in the kitchen? Gill? Fancy helping me butcher a hog?"

Gill's eyes lit up in a way Alex had only seen once before. "Oh yes, I would like that a lot," he blurted excitedly.

Gill and George rushed off. Jim, Brath, and Vardis continued standing in the living room, looking at their hands and trying to figure out what they should do. Alex said, "You guys should go help in the kitchen too."

Liza walked over to the huddle of boys, threw her arms around them, and exclaimed, "We're all helping. I can rustle up something for you to do."

As Liza ushered the boys into the back, Jollies flitted around her, begging Liza to tell her stories about her and her husband's exploits in VR. Liza laughed as she started to delegate tasks to the team, promising Jollies she would tell her all about them.

Alex watched as her two worlds blended seamlessly together. Chine probably would have fit in nicely as well if he could have fit into the house.

Liza and George instructed Alex's team and Vardis on how to set the table. Dinner hadn't taken too long to cook due to the many hands at work. Alex even offered a little bit of help, even though she was a terrible cook. Setting the table was something she knew like the back of her hand. She'd spent years doing it blind.

Once the table was set, she helped her family and her team cart the food out. She hadn't had human food cooked by human hands in a long time, and she had forgotten how much she loved her parents' cooking.

When they were all seated, Liza proposed a toast. She raised her glass of wine and said, "To new friends and new adventures. To the people who keep my daughter safe!"

Alex couldn't help smiling and looking at Jim. The night was going better than she could have imagined.

Across the table, Vardis reached for the pumpkin pie.

George clicked his tongue playfully as he passed the pie to Vardis. "You know, most places on Earth, you have to save dessert for last. Not in the Bound household, though."

Vardis smiled politely and nodded. "I greatly appreciate your hospitality. The last planets I have visited have not been..." He looked at Alex, who mouthed the word "normal."

"What I mean to say," Vardis continued, "is that this is a beautiful meal. Thank you."

Vardis cut a piece of pie and placed it on his plate. He

watched everyone eating for a second before grabbing his fork and cutting himself a bite. He tossed the pie into his mouth and chewed slowly. "Oh, that is delicious."

Suddenly, he screamed. His body convulsed, and his screams grew shriller.

Alex stood to go to Vardis when her head erupted in searing pain. She grabbed the back of her head as she lost her balance and fell to the floor. Whatever had happened to Vardis was happening to her as well.

CHAPTER FOUR

Alex couldn't see anything but red. The pain she felt was beyond anything she'd ever experienced. It felt like someone was slicing her open, starting at the spine, dragging the knife, taking their time, carving up her nerves until they got to her brain.

When Alex opened her eyes, she saw her family and friends crowding around her and Vardis, who was still screaming. She wanted to reach out, ask for their help, but she couldn't speak. Her jaw was clamped so tight she thought she was going to crack her teeth.

Another wave of pain wracked her, her back rigid as her hands clenched, frozen as if she were trying to hold onto something.

More pain, and still more. Her vision was starting to blur, the world around her fading. But not into darkness—into something more troubling and confusing. She watched herself on the floor, convulsing.

If Alex chose to look away, which she felt the strong urge to do, she could see stars flashing behind her as if they were rushing to be someplace. There were suns and moons, and they watched as Alex turned away from the small girl on the floor, quivering in agony.

Instead of staying, Alex walked through the cosmos, looking at whatever caught her attention. She was aware that the girl was still on the floor. So was the alien, but it didn't matter. The stars were more interesting.

Alex continued to wander, stopping here and there at an interesting planet, wondering what scurried across its surface or if it had life at all.

Then without warning, the universe went cold. It hadn't been warm before, but now it was freezing. Her bones ached from the sudden temperature drop. She hoped the girl she'd left behind was going to be safe.

She headed in the direction of the vicious breeze.

It was not long until Alex found what she was looking for. There was a small boy, pale as the whitest snow, wearing a fox-skin robe that reached his bare feet and a mask made from a deer's skull. The cold was not coming from the boy, though. It emanated from what he was staring at.

Ahead of him was something like a planet but nothing like one at the same time. It had mass, but the surface swirled and moved as if the skin were revolting against itself. Occasionally tendrils of the black skin-like substance shot out from the planet as if it were grasping for something around it.

The cold came from the thing.

As Alex watched the living black planet, she saw it shudder and expand. The expansion was slight, and as it grew larger, everything around it grew colder for a second as if it were sucking out the life of all that surrounded it.

Alex did not know why, but she wanted to reach out to the black planet, wanted to touch its slippery skin. She knew what would happen if they were to touch. It was a visceral knowledge, something that had been within her since birth and perhaps existed in all sentient beings.

Whatever that thing was, it would kill Alex if she touched it like it was killing that planet. One touch was all it would need. The black wasn't part of the planet, it was the thing that was killing it, and it could spread easily.

While Alex was drawn to the planet, she was also disgusted. Whatever had caused this to happen was unnatural. It disturbed her on a primal level. If she'd had a body, she probably would have been sick to her stomach. *Oh yeah, my body,* she thought absentmindedly, looking over her shoulder as if she would see it trailing behind her.

The little boy ahead turned to face Alex, his eyes glowing white-hot behind his mask. "What are you doing here? I didn't think I would see you again."

Alex heard the boy, but she had no idea what he was talking about. She stared at him blankly, wondering if that was his body or if he was like her—something outside of a body, floating about, trying to make sense of the universe in which it was merely a speck. "I don't know," she admitted. "I'm not sure what I'm doing here, either."

The boy pointed to the planet being swallowed up by a darkness vast and perverse. "That's what he does. That's how he eats them, and he wants to eat them all."

"The Eater of Worlds." Vardis had used that phrase to describe the Dark One. She had thought he was speaking metaphorically. He had explained how the Dark One took a planet's resources. Alex hadn't realized he meant the Dark One quite literally devoured planets from the inside.

What exactly *was* the Dark One? How could something that inhuman be able to control armies or create technology? What Alex was looking at right now didn't seem to have any more intelligence than lichen or a fungus.

Then something changed on the planet's surface. The

earth broke apart, swirling as if caving in on itself, and something forced itself from the opening rent. Teeth lined the gash as something like a fetus forced itself out of the planet's wound, its body frail and skeletal, its head encased in a shroud of some sort as clouds gathered, covering the thing's obscene nakedness.

An eye opened in the caul. It was large and angry, and it turned its cyclopean gaze upon Alex.

The thing knew she was there. It had seen her. She was terrified.

The thing snarled, its tendrils pulsing as they caressed the surface. Another blast of cold hit them as the planet grew larger.

A voice called to Alex from the darkness far behind her, back where the body of the girl and the strange alien were laying. *Alex!* it shouted. *Alex, come back!*

Alex recognized the voice. It was Chine. What was he doing out here? Dragons couldn't survive in space. Not without special equipment. She realized she couldn't survive in space without special equipment either. How the hell was she out here?

Come back, Alex! Come back now!

Alex didn't know if she should listen to the voice. Even though she was afraid of the thing clawing its way out of the tendril-filled planet, she knew it wouldn't hurt her. Or at least, she thought it wouldn't hurt her. She wasn't like the rest of space. She was like the pale boy. Where had he gone?

Then without warning, Alex felt hands on her back. They pulled her hard, and she fell back into the body of the girl who was lying on the floor. Her eyes had rolled back, and she was as rigid as a corpse.

Alex, back in her body, bolted upright fast enough to make everyone in the living room jump. Blood was pouring from her nose and her ears, and she felt sick to her stomach.

When she tried to move, she fell over and coughed up a bloody black mass of something she would have preferred not to look at. Then she passed out.

When Alex woke up, she was bundled in a blanket on the living room couch. Vardis was also wrapped in a blanket in her dad's chair on the other side of the room. Liza and Gill were in the room, both of them looking worriedly at the rider. "What happened?" she groggily mumbled.

Liza rushed over and covered Alex's forehead with kisses. "I didn't think my pumpkin pie was that bad," she managed to joke.

Alex laughed, but her stomach clenched, cutting her laughter off abruptly. "Your pie could never be bad enough to do that."

Across the room, Vardis was staring at Alex with his deep, dark eyes. Gill was doing the same, but his gaze was much softer and worried as well. "It was an attack," the alien said. "By the Dark One."

Alex tried to sit up. Her body ached less, and she felt like she needed to start moving to ease her muscles' cramps. "Why the hell would he attack me like that?" she asked. "He shouldn't even know I'm here."

"The attack was not on you, it was on me. As I told you before, we are linked psychically. I did not know that if someone invaded my mind to inflict harm on me, it would also affect you."

Alex rubbed her head as she tried to focus. Everything still felt very fuzzy. "Wait, are you saying the Dark One knows you're here?"

Vardis shook his head as he made a futile attempt to stand. "No, he does not. The Dark One is a powerful psychic.

He does not need to know where I am to find me. All he needs to do is search out my mind. Usually, there are defenses up. Unfortunately, the meal provided to me was so delicious that I let my guard fall. It will not happen again."

There were still things that didn't make sense to Alex. "How come it stopped? If he caught you off-guard and I can't defend myself, why did we all of a sudden stop being attacked?"

Vardis glanced at Gill, who was crouched in a chair, watching Alex closely. "Your friend did something he has yet to inform me about."

When Gill spoke, it was with the measured attention to detail and pronunciation that Alex had started to realize stemmed from a lack of trust. "I connected your mind to Chine's," the drow said, "using my own. I amplified the telepathic link between you and the dragon until he was able to help you."

Alex knew Chine had the ability to sense when she was in danger, but that was only good up to a certain amount of distance, and she was far beyond it. "Wait, are you saying you're psychic too?" Alex asked, suddenly realizing what Gill was implying. She could see why he would have wanted to keep that a secret.

Gill tapped the side of his head as he slowly shook it. "No, I am not. There are some abilities that drow possess that I have, and one of them is the ability to increase the innate abilities of those around me."

Liza's face brightened as she realized there was something she understood. "Kind of like buffs in VR, right?"

"Exactly. All I did was amplify the connection you and Chine already have. It's something I unconsciously do all the time, making Jollies more charming, Jim more adventurous, things like that. This was the first time I've tried to direct it, though."

Alex half-wondered what Gill was amplifying about her when she was around, but that could wait for another time. "So, that was Chine who pulled me out of there?"

"Exactly."

Alex looked around the room as she tried to hold everything together in her head. Her mind was still swimming. "Okay, now we know the Dark One can attack Vardis from anywhere. What do we do about it?"

Gill came over and sat next to Alex. "We move the plan up. We find this weapon and end this once and for all."

Alex looked at her mom, trying to force a smile. "Sorry dinner got ruined, but we'll have another one once this mission over. The next time, I won't get attacked by a psychic planet."

Liza hugged Alex, holding her tightly as she ran her hands through her daughter's hair. "Be safe, sweetie. If that thing can hurt you like that here, you need to get rid of it as fast as possible. I'm so proud of you."

Alex managed to pry herself away from her mom and stood. "Gill, get everyone ready. Time to put in an end to this."

CHAPTER FIVE

Team Boundless arrived at the base before nightfall. They were all tense. No one had spoken much about what had happened at Alex's home. There wasn't much to say. It made her uncomfortable.

An explanation outside of Vardis' would have been appreciated. It wasn't that Alex didn't trust the alien, she thought. Instead, it was that she was used to having information fed to her by Myrddin and Roy. She had to admit she'd been caught up in the chain of command. Having to think for herself in this situation was more than she'd expected.

That was not to say she was bitter about it. Initially, taking orders had been difficult for Alex. She'd have preferred to think for herself. Now she had to admit that there was a lot of comfort in knowing Myrddin usually had the answers.

Maybe Chine had something to help her get a better understanding of the situation. He was linked to her mind, and a strong enough telepath to pull her out of whatever that attack had been. There was a chance he might have learned something from the attack.

Team Boundless met Manny in the stables. He looked stressed out, all of his eyes whirling in a frantic way that made Alex uncomfortable. She hated seeing Manny stressed. He was incapable of hiding it, and naturally, it ended up freaking Alex out.

The dragons were already on the augment platforms. They had been outfitted with an apparatus that Alex had never seen before. There were tubes stretching from the dragons' mouths and wrapped around their backs, ending at the spinal anchor each of them was fitted with.

Goggles had also been attached to the dragons' eyes. Something that looked like an exoskeleton was being attached to their wings. It created the effect of having the bones of their wings on the outside, making them look bat-like.

Alex walked up to Manny as the rest of the team moved toward their dragons. "What's all this?"

Manny hardly looked up from his paperwork, floating back and forth. Alex hated it when he did that. The Beholder's anxiety was so intense that it was contagious. "What's what?" he mumbled distractedly.

Alex gestured to Chine, who was fidgeting uncomfortably as human scientists fiddled with the tubes that had been inserted in his mouth.

Manny glanced up for a second before returning to his paperwork. "Oh, that? We've had to adjust for the dragons being in space. I don't understand it all. You're going to have to get the technicians to explain it to you. And I need you to explain some things to me."

"You heard about what happened at dinner?"

His main eye gave Alex all his attention. "Of course, I heard about it." Manny sighed. "Gill and Jim both reported it as soon as it happened. But neither of them was very clear about what was happening, so I expect you to fill in the details."

Alex hoped she had a good enough understanding of what had happened to give Manny a satisfactory report. Truth be told, she was a little confused. She knew she'd been attacked telepathically by the Dark One due to her connection with Vardis, but she wasn't certain what the attack constituted.

Her body had been in pain, but at the same time, she'd been outside of it. That was the part that was confusing to her.

Alex figured it was best to just tell Manny what she'd experienced. "Vardis was attacked by the Dark One. I was dragged into it as well because we have a link. A psychic one."

All of Manny's eyes focused on Alex. "Does Myrddin know about the connection?"

Alex shifted her weight from foot to foot. "Yeah, he does. He wasn't happy about it. Made him more uncomfortable than I am. But we're linked together. I guess whatever hits him telepathically hits me as well."

"What happened? Jim said you were in a lot of pain."

Alex tried to find the right words, but there weren't any. "I was, at one point. My body was in pain, but my mind was detached. I was watching something. A planet. It was covered in some kind of black stuff, and then something like a baby came out of the planet and looked at me, but I don't know if it saw me. That was what was hurting me."

Alex took a second to think and see if she was forgetting anything important. "And that kid, the one I saw in the meteor? He was there as well. He said he was part of the Dark One."

"He was the one who helped you blow up the meteor, wasn't he?"

Alex thought back to what had happened then. She was

annoyed that she couldn't remember nearly as much as she wanted to. Was her mind intentionally hiding things from her?

After an extended period of silence while Manny waited patiently, Alex finally said, "I don't know if he was trying to help me. At the time, that's what seemed like, but now I don't know. Everything is confusing, and it's not like when I experience things in real life. I can remember those, and they don't confuse me. But what happened on the meteor or just now? That feels like trying to remember a dream. Everything starts to fade, or it doesn't make any sense."

Manny's eyes softened, showing that he was at least trying to understand. Whatever was happening with Alex was outside his experience. "Wait!" she suddenly exclaimed. "Can't you see multiple realities or dimensions or something like that?"

A few of Manny's eyes turned their attention back to the papers floating in front of him as if he were avoiding the conversation. "Yeah, I can. It's not as simple as you're probably thinking, but I can perceive dimensions and realms outside the one I'm currently in."

"Wherever I was, it wasn't this dimension. I don't know how I know that, but it wasn't. If you were linked with Chine and me, do you think you could tell me where it was? What I was seeing?"

Manny rubbed his chin with one of his eye tendrils. "It depends if I've seen it before. Most of the universe across the realms looks the same, even in other dimensions. Unless there was something very noticeable, like a dozen black holes or maybe a few dying stars next to each other—anything like that—I might be able to, if I've seen it before."

Alex thought back to her vision. There was nothing interesting or notable except the planet the Dark One was destroying. No landmarks she could think of. "Do you think it's worth a try?"

Manny thought it through. "Maybe you should talk to the technicians. There are some things you need to know about how the lack of gravity is going to affect your mission. After that, we'll give it a try."

Alex agreed with him. She did want to know where the Dark One was or if it was only a trick of the mind, but the mission at hand took priority. If Boundless was able to retrieve the weapon, it wouldn't matter either way. The Dark One would be dead. Problem solved.

With that in mind, Alex went over to the technician who was working on the space augments being attached to Chine. "I heard I'm supposed to get a tutorial on all this," she called as she approached.

The technician, a young man with dusty brown hair wearing a name tag that read Greg, turned to face Alex. "Hey, I've been waiting for you," he chirped cheerfully. "Glad to see you made it in time for me to go over everything. It won't take too long, I promise."

Greg waved Alex over and started to go through the augments he'd attached to Chine and why. The augments were far past the prototype stage but hadn't been tested with riders on dragons. He assured her that the important components were all safe.

The tubes that had been attached were to deal with the lack of oxygen in space. They'd been trying to figure out a way to get oxygen to the dragons before realizing that the dragons would be able to breathe their own nitrous oxide. The tubes were basically a funnel, taking the fumes that were in the dragons' stomachs and cycling them back through their systems, negating the need for them to carry oxygen.

The only problem was that the dragons would not be able

to use flame attacks. That meant their riders were going to have to be meticulous in the augments they chose.

Chine and the other dragons were not used to being without gravity, but according to Greg, that wasn't going to be the hard part.

The dragons weren't going to be able to use their wings. Thrusters were being added to their backs, which the riders controlled. If something went wrong, the dragons could operate them, but Greg wasn't sure how much good that was going to do.

Alex wished they had started training with these new controls weeks ago, or at least earlier in the day. It had been great to see her parents, but the time would have been much better spent getting used to the new way of riding.

Greg assured Alex that it would be like second nature in space. He did caution that it was going to take a lot more concentration since Chine wouldn't be able to help her when it came to control unless she completely relinquished hers. *Great,* Alex thought before reaching out to Chine and asking him if he was comfortable with the new equipment.

Chine chuckled. *Does it matter? Either way, this is our mission. We are going to have to do the best we can. We'll figure it out.*

Alex was glad the dragon was comfortable with the idea of being in space and having no control over his body. She wished she could pick up on his emotions more, but she realized that if Chine was very uncomfortable with the prospect, she would feel it. It would be nice to trust herself as much as Chine did.

Greg continued explaining the different augments she could use this time. She was only half-listening, though. Weapons were important, but they were something both she and Chine could easily figure out. She *was* concerned about why Greg was going on so long about how to arm up. Wasn't this meant to be a simple fetch quest?

Alex asked him, "What's the deal with all the weapons talk? When we were getting ready for a full-on invasion, nobody briefed us this much on artillery. This isn't supposed to be a dangerous mission from what I understand."

Greg seemed taken aback by the question. "Vardis didn't tell you? He said the area he hid the weapon is heavily armed. It shouldn't be a problem because he's got the codes to everything, but better safe than sorry, in my opinion."

Alex shut out the rest of what Greg explained. She focused on the fact that they were expecting to see heavy resistance on such a simple task—picking up a weapon. Something was off. Alex couldn't put her finger on it but, whatever it was, it had to do with Vardis.

There was no time to deal with doubts at the moment, though. The mission was a go. Once Greg finished lecturing Alex on the different things to pay attention to, Alex went to her teammates and briefed them on the possible complications. No one seemed to be surprised. Now that everyone was up to speed, Alex went and found Manny.

The Beholder was still dealing with his paperwork but looked much less bothered than before. "Finished with all the prep?"

Alex shrugged, not knowing what else to do. "This is starting to sound like much more than Vardis suggested. I want to see if you can help me pin down where the Dark One's attack came from."

Manny stretched out one of his tentacles to Alex. "Take hold of this."

Months ago, the notion would have disgusted Alex, but she'd grown up a lot. She grabbed it, and the Beholder's eyes rolled back as he tried to see what Alex had seen.

After a couple of seconds, Manny opened his eyes again.

"They are really from the same dimension. I can see that much."

Alex let go of his tentacle. At least that part was true.

An alarm sounded in the stables; it was time to head out. Alex wished she had more time. She wasn't certain what she was about to walk into, but she didn't feel prepared. But how was that different from anything else she'd experienced?

CHAPTER SIX

The dragons were set to take off at six in the evening. Tensions were high on the base. Alex didn't need to be told this was the first time dragons had been sent into space. True, they had gotten pretty close when Boundless had dealt with the meteor, but this was an entirely different beast.

Manny assured the riders that the whole thing would go smoothly. This wasn't something they had whipped up on a whim. Myrddin and the human base had been preparing for dragonriders to go to space since the inception of the program.

The last thing Boundless had to do was get their new gear. They would be holding onto their dragon anchors, but the armor they had used before would be useless. Someone in the DGA department (Alex suspected it was Abby and her crew) had figured out an ingenious way to use the draconic fluid in the anchors to supplement oxygen.

That meant that dragonriders wouldn't have to wear bulky spacesuits. They would be going into space with suits that were designed to deal with extreme temperatures.

The suits were self-regulating and would keep the rider's

body temperature optimal by supplementing the rider's metabolism with draconic fluid. The only downside was that the riders wouldn't be able to use the more powerful personal augments that relied on the draconic fluid.

Alex didn't think that would be a problem since there shouldn't be any fighting. The additional augments the dragons had been outfitted with were merely a precaution. Vardis had repeated multiple times that he could easily turn off the defenses around the weapon.

Vardis still hadn't disclosed what kind of weapon it was. That annoyed Alex, but the alien had assured her that explaining it would be a waste of time. The weapon was something that worked on an entirely different plane of reality, and Alex wouldn't be able to grasp the explanation of what it was or what it did.

She still thought it was fishy that it had been stored on her plane, but she knew little to nothing about quantum mechanics or multiple dimensions. For the time being, she resolved to keep her mouth shut and see what happened.

Myrddin still hadn't contacted Alex, and it was making her anxious. This was the first mission she was heading up, and she wished that he had at least left her something to work with. Granted, it meant Myrddin trusted her, but she wouldn't have turned down some hand-holding.

Once Boundless had had their suits refitted, they went back to the stables to prepare for the launch. Jim was talking nervously to Jollies, joking much more than usual while Brath and Gill had grown quiet, speaking only in small bursts about unrelated things.

Alex stopped the group outside the stables. "How's everyone feeling about this?"

No one in Boundless seemed to be in a rush to speak up. Finally, Gill said, "'Uncomfortable' would be the best way to put it."

"And what's got you feeling that way? I don't want to head up there until everyone has their heads on straight."

Gill looked over his shoulder as if he were worried that someone was listening in. "For one, this is all new tech we're using. None of us has tested it. Secondly, we are also going to be using this tech in a completely new environment. I don't know anything about Earth, and I know even less about your solar system."

Alex could see Gill's points, but those were things neither she nor anyone else had control over. "We all have gravity on our planets. So, we all should have a pretty good idea of what happens when we don't, right? But the rest of it, you're right about. This is new tech, which means we all have to be paying close attention."

Brath was bristling in his beard, tapping his fingers on his waist as he tried to contain whatever was going to inevitably come out. "Why are we even doing this?" he blurted. "If it's as simple as picking something up, they should be sending someone else."

Jollies' eyes went wide as she stared at Brath. "What? Do you think this is beneath us?"

The gnome started to pace, trying to burn off nervous energy or irritation. "No, I don't think this is beneath us. I'm just saying, the Nest has people pick up packages all the time. Some of them are pretty damn important. Why the hell are we suddenly delivery boys?"

Alex had been wondering the same thing, going in circles in her head. There were good reasons for either argument. If the weapon was that powerful and dangerous, Boundless should definitely be escorting it. Something that important couldn't be left to just anyone to take care of.

But Boundless wasn't the most qualified for the job even if that was the case. Why wasn't Myrddin here personally? If this thing could get rid of the Dark One once and for all, shouldn't he be retrieving it?

On the flip side, if there were defenses that could easily be disabled by Vardis, why didn't the Nest send one of the other platoons? Theoretically, anyone could do this job.

Alex didn't have the answers, and she didn't pretend to. "Look, I don't know. We have our orders. That's all I can say."

Gill cleared his throat as he checked over his shoulder again. "Maybe we should begin to question those orders?" he asked softly.

The members of Boundless seemed caught off-guard by Gill's words. It was not that it hadn't been thought of before. No one expected it to be Gill to say it, though. But he wasn't finished. "There are things going on that we don't understand. And it's our lives at stake. I refuse to be a pawn."

Alex could understand why he felt that way. It was how she'd felt when she'd realized Myrddin was keeping her in the dark, but things were different now. Or were they? "How does everyone else feel about this?"

Jollies and Jim, who had not spoken, exchanged glances, perhaps trying to figure out who was going to agree or disagree with Brath and Gill. Naturally, the pixie couldn't contain herself. "I don't like it," she blurted. "We never know what's going on. Ever. Why are they keeping us out of the loop?"

Jim countered, "That's the way the military works. They don't explain everything to every soldier. Do you know how much time that would waste? My dad was telling me that the amount of direct contact and intel was more than he ever had back when he was serving."

Brath glared at Jim and spat, "So your father was happy being a pawn in events he didn't understand?"

Jim's face darkened as he clenched his jaws and his fists.

"My dad is a great man. If you think you can talk about him—"

"I don't understand why humans have the desire to follow someone and never ask any questions. Are you all that stupid? Just because there's someone telling us that we have to do something, it doesn't mean we should. We don't have any idea what's going on half the time. They tell us to go kill this, get that, but we don't know why."

Jim squared up with Brath, both of them looking as if they were ready to draw their weapons. "You think Myrddin is pulling some double-agent crap?" Jaws growled. "You think we're all in some stupid-ass conspiracy or some shit?"

Brath stepped up to Jim, looking intimidating despite only coming up to Jim's waist. "I'm saying if you can't see that some of this doesn't make sense, you're either blind or an idiot!"

Gill stepped between the two and pushed them away from each other. "Everyone needs to calm down," he said. "All of us. This isn't the time or the place."

Both Brath and Jim looked like they could have punched Gill in the face, but they both backed down.

Alex knew she should step in, but she didn't know what to say. She wanted to back Jim, but she agreed with Brath. It felt like they needed to start questioning what was going on, but choosing a side right now wouldn't help anyone. Boundless needed to be a team.

"So, we all have problems with what's going on, right?" Alex cut in. "That's not changing what we're doing—"

Brath was still staring daggers at Jim, but he eased up as he turned his attention to her. "Alex, I'll be straight up with you. I didn't like you when I met you, but you're a good leader. One of the best I've ever seen. And I'll follow you. But you need to know, I want to trust you. And if you're just doing whatever you're told without asking questions, how can I do that?"

For the first time since Alex had met Brath, she could see the vulnerability in his eyes. He was scared. Terrified. And she could see why. She just wasn't sure what to make of it. Instead of asking Gill, who she knew would give an answer that was mired in coolness and logic, she turned to Jollies, and asked, "What do you think?"

The pixie glanced at the different members of Boundless, no doubt trying to take emotional cues from them. When she couldn't find anything, the color of her skin shifted to a near-translucent hue, showcasing her veins and vital organs. "We're following *you*, Alex. Not Myrddin," she said softly.

The rest of Boundless remained silent, each of them going through what their various statements meant.

Alex was also silent, trying to grasp the loyalty Boundless was giving her. "Fine. If that's the case, we're doing this. I don't know anything more than the rest of you. We finish this mission, and then we stop taking every order that comes down to us. If it's important enough for us to risk our lives, then we should know everything possible about it. Deal?"

The rest nodded in agreement.

"Good," she said. "Now, let's get this over with."

CHAPTER SEVEN

Most of the base's personnel were gathered in the stables. This was a momentous occasion, the first dragons going in space. Alex wondered what that meant to the people watching. For most of them, this was the first time they'd ever seen a dragon. What did it matter if they were going to space?

In a small corner of her mind, Alex felt ashamed of being judgmental. It wasn't long ago that she'd never seen a dragon. Then again, it wasn't long ago she couldn't see anything at all. Of course, they should be excited. It would be weird if they weren't.

Alex knew where the sneaky judgment came from too. She was annoyed. Not with Boundless, not with Brath. Everything that had been said was true. But it still bothered her. What good was an authority like Myrddin or anyone else if you couldn't trust them?

Trust wasn't something Alex had ever had a problem with. Her parents had always been straightforward with her. They'd never hidden anything from her or played games. Even when Alex had run off to try to save the nine realms, her parents had invested in the very thing that caused her to make that decision.

Not being able to trust Myrddin or anyone else in charge was a new concept for Alex, and it made her feel extremely unsettled.

She and the rest of Boundless seemed to have had something sucked out of them. This should have been an exciting mission, one most kids would have given anything for. But here were four teenagers, unable to look to the stars with any semblance of joy.

Manny came up behind Alex as she stood in front of Chine's platform, looking at his augments. She had allowed the maintenance team to take care of them. She wasn't sure what would be more useful in space. They'd informed her that the dragon's flames wouldn't be available due to the breathing apparatus. Machine guns and missiles were also not usable due to the lack of gravity.

At that point, Alex had no idea what weapons were viable, so she left it up to those who knew better and asked to be given a comprehensive explanation of what she had. She wanted to kick herself for not coming to the stables earlier and taking a look at the list.

Manny floated between Alex and the computer terminal. "You guys ready to do this?" he asked with a huge smile on his face.

Alex was certain the smile was genuine. Could Manny be trusted? She stared blankly at the smile. No, not Manny. She'd seen how much he was willing to risk for her and the others. There was no way she couldn't trust Manny.

"About as ready as you can be to shoot off into space," Alex answered. "Everything looking good down here?"

"I'm asking the same thing. You guys okay? You look a little distracted."

Alex glanced over her shoulder at the rest of the riders

prepping their dragons and getting ready to leave. "I think we're just nervous," she said, regretting lying to him. Maybe she could tell him the truth. Maybe it would be helpful to have someone on their side.

Their side? Are you serious, Alex? It isn't them against us. We're all trying to do the same thing—get rid of the Dark One.

Yeah, but some of us are fighting, and others who have the power to destroy entire armies are sitting up in their ivory castles, letting us take all the risks.

Alex knew that wasn't fair. Myrddin was practically running the whole war effort. Still, thinking about it stung.

All of those worries and fears could be set aside for the moment. Alex pushed them down with everything else she'd been forcing out of her head for the last few months. She knew it was all going to come up at some point—it didn't take a degree in psychology to figure that out—but it wouldn't be today. *Chine, you ready to do this?*

The dragon stood up as smoke rose from his nostrils. *Let's hurry up and take care of this,* he growled in Alex's head. *I want to get out of this thing as soon as possible. Tubes in your stomach? Humans have to figure out less barbaric ways to accomplish their goals.*

Chine was uncomfortable, and his lizard-like face showed his pain. *We won't drag this out, big guy,* Alex said as she jumped onto his back.

Alex attached her anchor and felt her boots connect with the dragon's back. The connection was stronger than usual. On Middang3ard, Alex could walk around on Chine if she wanted to. That wasn't going to happen this time. She could tell her feet weren't going anywhere.

Jollies came through on Alex's comm. "You know, we're behind you, right?" she asked. "Everything we were saying, it isn't about you. None of it. You're a rider like us."

"Yeah, I know," Alex replied. "I appreciate you telling me, though."

"Brath wanted to say something, but he couldn't bring himself to. I mean, not to you. He's been muttering about it to Gill since we've started suiting up."

"What about Jim?"

Jollies didn't answer immediately. "Uh, he hasn't really said anything."

"Are you just telling me that?"

Alex could hear the hurt in Jollies' voice. "Of course not! I just wasn't sure what would have been better—if he had said something or he hadn't. Either way, he hasn't said anything."

Alex looked at the open sky above her. "It's probably better that way. We shouldn't have any infighting going on. Thanks for being a bigger person than Brath."

"Not a problem."

The gnome's surly voice growled through the comm, "You know, you never disconnected from me, Jollies."

The pixie squeaked, "Oh, crap! Uh, gotta go, Alex!"

Despite her stress and unease, Alex couldn't keep herself from chuckling as she prepared for takeoff. Even if everything was crazy around her, she at least had her team. That was the important thing. Nothing was going to break Boundless up. "All right, everyone," she shouted. "Get ready for takeoff!"

Alex pivoted her foot slightly and then pulled up hard on her dragon anchor, activating the thrusters on Chine's back.

She instantly saw what the technicians had meant by her needing to take a lot more control of the dragon. There was noticeable resistance when she pulled her anchor back. Turning would be difficult.

But the thrusters worked fast. Chine was already rising in a fashion not much different than Jim's mech, which was also starting to ascend. The rest of the riders were lifting off as well. Alex could hear them muttering over the open channel they usually kept open once everyone was airborne. "Oh, I don't like this!" Gill said.

On the other hand, Brath was cackling. "Are you serious? Furi loves this." He laughed. "Do you see how big these thrusters are? We could really haul ass if we wanted to. Plus, this guy is overjoyed that he practically gets to sit this one out. Just a big ol' boat, right?"

Alex tuned out the rest of the riders. Not because she wasn't interested or didn't want to joke, but she really wanted to get a handle on what this ride was going to be like. She'd already noticed an increased amount of tension, and Brath had mentioned how strong the thrusters were.

There was only one way to figure that out.

Alex rotated her hand, instinctively changing the direction of the thrusters and punched forward. They launched at full throttle, rocketing into the sky with a force unmatched by anything humanity had sent to the stars to date.

She looked over her shoulder and watched the base disappear in a matter of seconds. "Holy crap!" she shouted as she slowed down, waiting for Boundless to catch up with her. She hadn't been expecting to move *that* fast. "This thing is like a hyperdrive!" She laughed.

The riders had nearly caught up. Alex couldn't help but wonder what Jollies' and Amber's speed was like. They were the faster riders by a long shot.

"Not quite hyperdrive," a voice said.

Alex looked around and saw that Vardis had joined them. He wasn't using a ship, though. He was merely flying through the sky, a bright yellow aura around him. As if reading Alex's mind, which he probably was, he said, "Your atmosphere is much thinner than I'm accustomed to. I can easily keep pace with you and your dragons for our trip to the moon."

Just how strong is this guy in our dimension? Alex thought, becoming increasingly aware that Vardis might be able to read all of her thoughts. It made her very uncomfortable.

Chine's voice came through Alex's head. *Don't worry about Vardis. He might be a powerful telepath, but he's nothing compared to me. As long as I'm conscious and we're this close, he won't hear anything. Nothing like what happened at dinner could occur right now.*

Alex heaved a sigh of relief. *I'm glad to hear that.*

This was the fun part—breaking through the atmosphere. Alex knew how powerful the thrusters were, but she didn't see the point in pushing them to their limit again. Instead, she started a steady ascent, paying close attention to how each movement between her and Chine felt, while also allowing herself to enjoy the new sensation of flight.

Having this much control was different. It felt more like what she'd experienced in VR. Very familiar, but not as good as the real thing. Still, she was glad it wasn't completely foreign. She could still enjoy the experience.

And what an experience. It only took one look over her shoulder at the Earth disappearing behind her to make her heart swell. Everything she'd known in her earlier life had become small.

As the air started to thin, Alex felt the dragon anchor start to heat up. That must have been the oxidation of draconic fluid to oxygen. *Thank God for magic tech,* Alex thought. *Gonna have to shoot Abby an email about this one.*

The stars got much larger. One moment, Alex was very aware she was still in the Earth's atmosphere, and the next, they weren't. She felt the last bit of gravity relinquish them, and there was a moment when she felt her body rising as if she'd float off of Chine. Then the anchor kicked in, and she settled down on his back again.

What a sight it was—an infinity of blackness peppered with lights that twinkled and invited. It was beyond anything

Alex could ever have imagined. It must have been the same for the rest of the riders and dragons because they were all silent.

"This is so beautiful," Jollies finally said. "Incredible."

Alex nodded before she realized she was still capable of talking. "Yeah. I can't wait to see the moon," she finally said. "Let's go, Boundless."

CHAPTER EIGHT

Team Boundless raced toward the dark side of the moon. They were all silent, thoroughly engrossed by the foreign beauty of space. For all their lives, they had stared at the sky at night. Alex didn't think any of them had ever dreamed they'd be up there.

Crossing into different realms had been exciting, but there was no comparison. The realms were mirrors of one another. Nothing was very different or alien. Space was something else entirely.

Alex activated her HUD and started to record everything she could see. Her parents would lose their minds over this. It would be a nice memory to look back on after the Dark One was taken care of. *"Hey, remember that time I went to outer space?"*

The moon was getting closer. It was time to focus on the mission at hand. "Vardis, where are we going?" she asked. "Did you send us specific coordinates?"

Vardis came up on Alex's side and shook his head. "No, it was dangerous to send them. If the Dark One had any spies in your base, I risked giving up the location. But I'll lead you there. Just follow me."

Vardis took point as Boundless began to swoop around the moon. The sheer size of it was humbling, and Alex couldn't help but stare at it in awe as they circled it.

As they went around the moon, Alex was relieved to see that "far side" was much more accurate than "dark side." She and her father had gotten into multiple arguments about what existed there, unseen by humanity.

Her father, being into conspiracy theories, believed there were alien bases on the part of the moon that was cloaked in darkness. Alex had tried to explain multiple times that the far side of the moon wasn't dark. It just couldn't be seen.

They had agreed to disagree. Alex was glad to see they were both right. That side of the moon definitely wasn't dark, and if there wasn't an alien base, there *was* a weapon hidden by an interdimensional being. That was pretty close.

Vardis led the team as they started to descend to the moon surface. Alex felt a little bit of gravity kicking in. That meant movement would be even more different than when they were flying in the void or in Earth's gravity. It was something she was going to have to take into account.

They landed, and Alex dismounted. Her suit compensated for the low gravity on the moon and weighed her down. She'd never seen videos of the moon landing, but her father had explained to her how ridiculous everyone had looked hopping around. Thank God that wasn't something she needed to stress about.

Vardis pointed at a massive crater Alex had seen when they had neared the surface. "There," he said. "That's where we'll find it."

Alex followed him, Chine right behind her with the rest of the dragonriders. "Why didn't we just land at the crater?"

"I wanted to give myself enough space to be able to deactivate the defense system. It can't be done from the above, only on the surface. An extra precaution."

They got closer to the crater, and finally, Vardis held up his hand and stopped. A datapad fizzled—that was the only word that worked—into existence in his hand. It was a different type of physical disruption than when Myrddin conjured something into existence. Whatever Vardis did looked like a small hole had been torn in his palm, and something had bubbled out like the fizz of opening a soda.

Vardis swiped through a couple of options and then looked at the crater. "That should have done it."

Gill came up behind Alex. "Which means that we are safe now?" he asked pointedly.

Vardis didn't seem to note or mind the tone of Gill's voice because he answered cheerfully enough, "Yes, we should all be safe now."

"What do you mean 'we?'"

"The defense system is set to attack, regardless of who enters. I will be in just as much danger as you if the system isn't deactivated."

Gill exchanged glances with Alex. Maybe they'd been wrong about Vardis. Either way, Alex was getting sick of the back and forth. If she wanted to deal with a lack of trust, she would have been a spy or something like that. All she wanted to do was know who the bad guys were and take care of them. Keep things simple. "Well, what are we waiting for?" she said.

She climbed back on top of Chine and Vardis led them to the crater, which was much larger than it had looked from space. It was easily the size of a small city block, jagged chunks of rock jutting into the sky, with ditches and scars the length of a football field. Something had torn into the moon's surface. Alex hoped she never found out what it was.

As Chine stepped into the crater, the air around them

shimmered. Alex almost didn't notice it, and she was certain that if she'd had regular eyes, she wouldn't have seen it. "Did any of you guys pick up on that?" she asked through the comm, glad Vardis wasn't on the channel.

Most of the riders said no, but Gill agreed that he had noticed something. It had been slight, and he'd thought his eyes were playing a trick on him, but if Alex thought she had seen something too, they had.

Vardis had stopped walking and was staring at the sky. "Oh no," he whispered.

Alex followed Vardis' gaze. The shimmer she'd seen when crossing into the crater was spreading throughout the sky in the shape of a dome, stretching to the other side. "That doesn't sound like a good 'Oh no,'" Alex shouted at him.

The alien slowly turned to face Alex, his jaw slack, his eyes wide with fear. "The security system," Vardis gasped. "It's been tampered with. It's still functional."

Before Alex could ask what that meant for them, the sky lit up as if someone had set off fireworks. She could see rocks streaking across the sky, and they were coming straight for them. "Scatter!" she shouted.

Boundless went in five directions, each of them moving slower than they would have if their dragons had control. But it was enough, and they separated in time to avoid the boulders as they collided with the surface of the moon, throwing up dust and debris everywhere so that there was a veil obstructing everything.

A deep hum was coming from where the rocks had landed. There was something in the blast zone. "What the hell kind of defenses do you have!" Jim shouted at Vardis.

The alien was backing away, his eyes wide with terror. "Something horrible."

As the dust settled, Alex narrowed her eyes, focusing to cut through the dust. She could see the rocks. There were three of them, and they were glowing a dull green, their surfaces pulsating as if they were egg sacs.

Then one of the boulders cracked, and something dark and wet slithered onto the ground. It looked almost like a snake, except it had hands and its tail was a stinger. The creature's head was a misshapen mass of tendrils that gave the illusion they were stacked on top of each other, one over the other in a mess.

The rest of the rocks cracked as well, the same sort of creature slithering from the green afterbirth as the first began to swell, its soft skin growing harder until, still growing faster than naturally possible, its tendrils and its skin developed a rock-like look as its arms stretched out, claws ripping from its fingertips.

Boundless regrouped around Alex and Vardis, who was still in the grip of terror. "Vardis, what in the nine realms are those?" Brath shouted.

"Elder kin," Vardis muttered. "Experiments of the gods from my realm. They... We must leave now. Otherwise, we are doomed."

Alex couldn't believe what was happening. "What are you talking about, 'leave?' We came here for the weapon!"

"If we leave before they notice us, they'll be contained to the sphere. The weapon will be lost, but at least no one else will be able to retrieve it."

Alex didn't know what to do. She wasn't sure if Vardis was right about anyone else being able to get the weapon.

And if the Dark One could get his hands on it, there was a chance he could use it against them. No, it was too risky. "Boundless, are you with me?" she shouted.

The team answered yes without hesitation.

"Good. We're going for that weapon. If it means cutting those things down, so be it."

Vardis stepped in front of Alex, panicked, waving his

hands. "No, you don't understand! These things are the stuff of gods! They'll rip you apart!"

Alex had Chine gently push Vardis out of the way. "Our mission is to get the weapon." Then she leaned forward, sending the dragon racing at the first creature as it turned its tendrilled head toward Boundless.

It rose into the sky, stretching out its long, craggy body. The thing moved as if it had no concept of gravity or perhaps even movement, contorting in bizarre ways as the rest of the monsters floated into the air.

For a second, Alex had the naïve idea that they wouldn't attack. However, once the kin stretched out its hand, Alex felt stupid for entertaining the thought.

It was hard to tell what it was doing at first. Its vaguely humanoid hands made some sort of gesture, then a beam of green light shot out at Alex.

Alex leaned hard to the right, yanking on her anchor, barely managing to pull Chine out of the way. She hadn't been expecting such a delay. On Middang3ard, that attack would have been nothing. She was really going to have to pay attention to what was going on.

Before she could formulate her next move, the creature was before her, its tendrils swirling as it looked into Alex's eyes.

Her terror was immediate. It was a fear Alex had only experienced one other time, in the depths of the meteor. It was enough to suck the warmth out of her body. But it hadn't broken her the last time. It wasn't going to break her now. "Two to a kin," Alex growled into her comm. "Vardis, you're with me."

Alex pulled her scythe from her anchor. She brought it down on the monster, whose body shifted out of reality for a second. When it phased back in, its rocky body wrapped around Chine, dragging him to the ground. Alex disengaged the gravity on her boots, jumped to the kin's head, and slashed at it.

The blade of her scythe hit the creature and it pulled back, releasing the dragon. It stared at Alex for a few seconds as if surprised that anything would dare to attack it. Then Alex felt the terror again. This time, she realized she wasn't afraid; the terror was radiating from it.

Jim and Jollies had linked up. Jollies was flying around the kin's body, trying to shock it with Amber's electrical jolts, but its skin seemed to be made of stone. There was no effect. Jim was sending flames at it but to no effect.

Brath and Gill weren't faring any better. Furi had tackled the kin to the ground, while Gill was trying to use Timber's rock elemental powers to cover it in stones thrown up from the moon's surface. When the stones touched the creature, it phased out, then popped back in, the stones now part of its growing body.

Alex watched as her opponent doubled back, its body shifting in and out of reality. Its tendrils waved wildly like the hands of one driven mad, grasping for some meaning for their insanity.

Alex needed to figure out effective tactics fast. Otherwise, this fight was going to be over before it began.

CHAPTER NINE

The three kin took to the air. There was no warning before they detached from the dragonriders and floated up toward the stars, hovering ominously above. "What are they doing?" Alex shouted at Vardis.

The alien, who still hadn't gotten himself together, stared up. "I have no idea," he muttered.

Great, Alex thought. The only way she was going to ensure Boundless came out of this alive was to stop relying on Vardis. He was useless in this situation he had created. "Boundless, figure out what you have aboard your dragons to take these things out. There's no way we were sent up here defenseless."

Alex looked at her dragon anchor, scrolling through the augments that had been attached to Chine. None of them looked familiar, and she couldn't tell what most of them did off the top of her head. All but one—she recognized an augment attached to Chine's left arm. It was a gravity well.

Above, the creatures were charging some kind of weapon. An energy beam was brightening in the middle of the circle they had formed as if they were summoning it into existence.

Alex wasn't going to wait for that to happen. She also wasn't going to storm into the fight without giving her team a heads up on what she was thinking about doing.

She readied the gravity well, interested to see what would happen in a place with less gravity than the last time she used it. "Okay, I hope that was enough time for you to figure out your augments. I'm going to disrupt the kin with a gravity attack. I'll scatter them. After they split apart, we're back to two on one. It must have been giving them a problem since they broke off for a group attack. We're keeping them separate from each other, okay!"

The members of Boundless shouted their approval.

Alex yanked up hard on her anchor and sent Chine flying through the air. She reached to Chine's left arm, accessing the gravity well and prepping it. Once she and her dragon got close enough, she fired the well.

The result was instantaneous. A large bubble about the size of a football, glowing brightly, shot toward the kin, landing in the middle of their circle. Then the well detonated, drawing all three of them forward with the sudden shift in gravity.

The creatures seemed to be caught off-guard by the attack, and they screeched as their bodies momentarily lost control. Alex took the opportunity to attack. Chine flew toward the monsters as Boundless prepared to launch their attacks.

Alex zoomed between the three kin, finding one to focus on. Chine tackled it, sending it careening away from the other two. He clamped down hard on its head.

The kin's tendrils wrapped around Chine's jaw, forcing it open. As Chine fought it, the kin grabbed the dragon by the throat and threw him to the ground.

Chine and Alex hit the ground with enough force to indent it. Before either of them could get back to their feet, the creature crashed into them, broadening the hole. If it weren't for the reinforced gravity from the anchor, Alex would have been thrown from Chine, who was roaring in pain.

The gravity well wasn't ready to be used again. Alex accessed the weapon on Chine's right arm. A beam of energy created a sword, and she slashed it across the monster's face.

The kin screeched and pulled back, shifting out of reality and appearing behind Alex. Before she could pull Chine around, it grabbed the dragon by the tail, hoisted him into the air, and slammed him into the ground again.

To Alex's left, Jollies and Jim were struggling with their kin as well. Jollies had implemented an energy field she was trying to encase the creature in while Jim was sending bursts of flame at it. It hardly seemed to notice either attack.

After Jollies had the energy field established, she flew back a little way to catch her breath. The kin should be encased for a moment, enough time to give Jim and her time to regroup.

Yet the kin phased out, then appeared outside the energy field. It went straight for Jollies, who turned and ran, pushing Amber as fast as she could. Jim flew after it, firing an energy beam cannon that came out of his mech's chest.

The kin merely shifted reality again, easily dodging the attack, then appearing behind Jim. Its tendrils wrapped around Jim's mech. It dove toward the surface of the moon, dragging Jim with it as Furi and Timber flew overhead, firing gravity attacks at the kin they were fighting.

Furi latched onto the kin's back with his claws, which began to heat up. Within seconds, Furi's claws were on fire.

Like the rest of them, this one didn't seem fazed by Furi's attack. It rolled to the side, heading for the ground, scraping Furi off. Then it sped up, whipping around and launching a beam attack at Timber, who was barely able to evade it.

Vardis yelled over his comm, "They have a weak spot! If you fire at their joints, the place where stone meets stone, it should split them apart!"

Alex relayed the information to the rest of Boundless, irritated that Vardis had only just found the guts to speak. He still hadn't joined the fight.

The gravity well was ready to be deployed again. So far, it had been Alex's most useful weapon. She leaned forward, sending Chine sprinting across the ground. The kin followed the dragon. Suddenly, Alex pulled up on her anchor, stopping Chine on a dime, allowing the monster to pass over the two of them.

Alex hit the gravity well and sent it at the kin, aiming for the joint between the sections of rock that covered its body. As the gravity well pulled at the creature, tearing away chunks of rock, Alex drew her scythe and sent it flying into the kin's joint.

At the same time, the rest of Boundless was trying to take advantage of the information they had just been given. Jim and Jollies had circled their kin, Jollies flying close and dropping electrical charges that attached to its joints while Jim distracted it by firing beams.

Brath and Gill were taking a different route. They were going for a contest of brute strength. Both Furi and Timber were on top of the kin, forcing it to the ground while the dragons tore at its joints, occasionally firing the ice beams attached to Timber's shoulders. Once the ice formed, both dragons slashed at the creature's weak spot.

Alex's kin screeched as it rolled out of the sky and crashed to the ground, where it skidded until it was still. Not wanting to give it any chance to get back up, Alex selected the plasma beams attached to Chine's shoulders. She fired at the kin's joints right below its head.

The plasma beam cut through, severing the head. "Yes!" she shouted.

Chine's voice rang through Alex's head a second later. *Wait! It is not time to celebrate yet.*

The tendrils stretched out and reattached the head to the body. Then it phased out of existence and reappeared behind Alex and Chine, and its tendrils hit the girl in the chest.

The air went out of Alex's lungs as she tried to hold onto Chine. The kin was too strong. She went flying off Chine's back as the monster wrapped more tendrils around Chine's body, trying to choke the dragon to death.

Alex hit the ground, skidding across and smashing her head against a rock. She stumbled to her feet, trying to keep from passing out. When she took a step forward, the creature phased into existence in front of her. It swiped at Alex with its claws, sending her flying again.

It reappeared above Alex and drove its claws into the ground, slamming her into the rock, then lowered its tendrilled head down to her still body as if to absorb her.

Alex groggily stared up into the tendrils that descended upon her in all their eldritch horror.

Before the tendrils could touch Alex, Chine tackled the kin from the right, sending the creature flying. Then he scooped Alex onto his back.

As Alex started to come to, she looked up. The same was happening to the rest of Boundless. They were unable to keep up. They all realized that the combination of such powerful enemies and being ill-prepared was resulting in a desperate situation, almost as if they had been set up. "We're not going to win this," Alex whispered.

Not through conventional means, Chine answered. *But there is a way.*

How? What are you talking about?

We use the gravity well to trap all the kin. Then I unleash my ether flames.

Alex leaned forward and rested her hand on the back of Chine's neck. *That would—*

Chine interrupted her. *Yes. It would detonate my breathing apparatus. I would die. You might too. But it would destroy the kin for sure. There is nothing in any dimension that can survive the pure flames of black ether, and they would be unable to escape if we used the gravity well.*

Alex chuckled morbidly. *You know, you have a habit of suggesting suicide as a way to achieve victory.*

Our friends will live through our sacrifice, and the weapon will be retrieved.

Alex checked the status of the gravity well. It was ready to be deployed. *You don't have to convince me. If all of us die here, no one's getting this weapon. Let's finish this.*

Alex had stared death in the face on the meteor with the Dark One. Back then, it had seemed like the most frightening thing in the world. Now, she was confused as to why she was so dull and hollow inside. Her life was about to be over, and all she could feel was faint resignation.

Maybe it's because you feel like this could have been avoided, she thought. *No, that's not going to help right now. Not at all.*

Alex hit her comm, patching to the rest of the dragonriders. "Riders, I want you to get away from your kin. Head toward me. You need to start putting distance between them and you."

Jim was the first one to speak. "Wait, what are you thinking about?"

"That's an order! Now get moving!"

Alex didn't wait to hear if Boundless disagreed. She fired energy at her kin to get its attention and then headed for the other two, charging the gravity well as she went. If this was going to be her and Chine's last attack, she figured it wouldn't hurt to dump all her anchor's energy into the well. The more, the better.

Ahead, the riders were doing exactly what Alex had told them to. They had caught the attention of their kin and were racing toward Alex.

Jollies and Jim passed her, Jim watching her as he went by. Alex wished she could have said more. Next were Brath and Gill. They both glanced at Alex, and she could see they knew what she was planning on doing.

Once the riders were out of the way, Alex activated the gravity well, aiming it at the two kin in front of her. As it fired, she pulled another scythe from her anchor and tossed it into the tendrilled mess that was the kin behind her.

The one following Alex sped up and hit both her and Chine, sending them into the gravity well as it exploded, creating a gravitational vortex that pulled all three monsters plus Alex and Chine into it.

They all went swirling around, Alex hardly able to tell where she and Chine began and the kin ended. "Are you ready for this?" the dragon asked.

Alex clenched her fist, feeling the draconic fluid boiling in her anchor. She slammed her fist to her chest, setting herself aflame as she drew her scythe again. *Torch 'em, Chine,* she sent as she leaped into the gravitational well, heading for one of the kin.

Chine let loose a torrent of ether flames. She'd only ever seen Chine use the attack from above, never this close. Beautiful black flames shot from his jaws.

The flames whirled through the gravitational vortex, converting the spinning bodies into a flaming tornado that stretched up to the sky. Alex could hear the kin screaming. She could distantly tell that she and Chine were screaming as well.

Alex hit the ground before she realized what had

happened. Chine was above her. He was badly burned but still on his feet, though he was struggling to breathe.

The vortex of flames surrounded them. They were in the eye of the storm.

Alex walked over to look Chine in the eye. She collapsed in front of him, and he picked her up. They stared at each other, neither capable of speaking, the little oxygen they had left fading from their lungs.

Above, in the ether flames, there was a spark of green light that erupted, changing the black flames to a sickly green.

Rider and dragon looked up at the green. It filled Alex with horror. And in the midst of that horror, Alex realized she was not ready to die, and she wasn't ready to watch Chine die either.

Alex ripped off her dragon anchor and tossed it to the ground. Her body erupted into flames, their black aura covering her, and she plunged her hand deep into Chine's body, tearing through his scales, straight to the hot draconic fluid that filled him.

The black flames around Alex grew stronger, covering both her and Chine, shooting up into the now-green vortex. Then there was only black.

CHAPTER TEN

She was in a blank place that held neither time nor space nor gravity. It was at once flat and filled with depth. Her feet were wet, and when she looked down at the water, it was pale green, as if it were a parody of life.

Calling. She was calling or screaming, but the intention was true. Someone had to find her. This wasn't where she was meant to be.

Chine was somewhere. His voice was loud but far away.

Alex took off running. She didn't know how or to where but she sprinted into the blank whiteness that stretched farther than her eyes could comprehend. The only sounds in this flattened non-reality were her footsteps and those of Chine, invisible somewhere in the whiteness.

Then the color shifted. Alex could see there was a deep-red sky, with black clouds filled with lightning. Everything else was a sickly green that crept into Alex's mind as she tried to focus on Chine's voice in her head.

Dustling. Dustling.

Alex was sinking in the water. She struggled as it sucked

her down. There was nothing to hold onto, nothing to breathe.

She shot out of the water into dryness and leaned forward, retching. Something slid out of her throat. When she looked down, it appeared to be a small snake, but instead of a snake's head, it was hers, eyes cracked and red, tongue lolling out like a tired dog's.

Alex slapped the obscene thing away as she stumbled to her feet, the world around her shifting and spinning. Chine's voice was still somewhere in the madness, but now there was another—a louder voice coming from behind. She had no desire to find out what else was here and took off toward the dragon's voice.

There was no measure for how long she ran, but she eventually came across Chine. The dragon was resting on a rock in the middle of a lake.

Alex swam out to him, and he picked up his head and stared at her. *I wasn't sure if you were here as well,* he thought.

Alex climbed onto the island and looked around. Above, there were thousands of moons and thousands of planets clustered together in the shape of a question mark. *Where are we?* she asked.

Chine pointed to the question mark. *Your guess is as good as mine. Someplace not too different than the meteor, I'm assuming.*

Do you think we are dead?

Chine pressed his hand down into the ground he rested on, watching how it separated so he could touch the water. *No, I do not think so. This is not what dragons who have passed through the veil and returned have described. This is something else. What, I do not know.*

"It is not death," a voice rang out.

Chine and Alex jumped to their feet. Walking on the

water was the pale child wearing a deer-skull mask. As the child strode toward Alex and Chine, something rose from the water.

The thing was tied to a tree that stretched up and far out into the infinity of the sky, its branches bare and weary. It seemed to be a person, unlike anyone Alex had ever seen before. Its skin was alabaster-white, and Alex could see veins and blood and muscles moving beneath it.

The thing's single eye was black, and she could not bring herself to look into its face. Its legs melded into the bark of the tree, its arms shaking as it coughed up black sludge and wailed in agony. Its torso pulled as if it were trying to escape from the tree. "Alex," it growled.

The child continued walking, ignoring the monstrosity leering behind it. "Alex," the child said. "I am so glad we found you. I've been trying to reach you for—"

Alex grabbed the kid, suddenly remembering everything that had happened in the meteor, everything she had tried to block out and forget. "What are you doing here? Is that him? You... We saved you! *Why are you with him again?*"

The child slipped from Alex's grip without any obvious movement. "That? That is not the Dark One, only a shade. One of millions, much like me. And we were wrong. I can never get away from him. Not completely."

Chine had maintained his calm, and he took Alex up in his hand as wildflowers sprouted across his scales. "Why have you brought us here?"

The child knelt in the water, watching his reflection. "I did not bring you here. This was a lucky coincidence. You both were near the veil and got caught up. It's the only time I've been able to speak to you without Vardis listening in."

Alex leaned over Chine's claw. "Vardis? Why are you trying to avoid him?"

The thing hanging from the tree moaned loudly, its body convulsing as it shouted, "Liar! Liar!"

The child looked at the thing on the tree for a moment before turning back to Alex. "He is not to be trusted. You and I have the same aim—to rid ourselves of the Dark One. Vardis' aim is less clear, but his means are false. The weapon he promised is not meant to destroy the Dark One. It is meant to destroy all of existence."

At these words, the thing nailed to the tree with roots that stretched through the stale water began to speak in a language Alex had never heard before. It tried to hold itself upright but failed and its head collapsed into its chest, the tree sucking itself in as well.

Alex climbed out of Chine's hand. "How can I trust you? Aren't you just a piece of the Dark One? A piece that apparently can't get away?"

The child stood up, its fingers still dripping from the lake. "The only way I will know release is through the Dark One's death. All I can do is warn you. What you do with that warning is up to you."

The child melted into water, leaving only the deer-skull mask.

Alex climbed back into Chine's hand and curled into a ball. "I hate this so much."

Chine opened his wings, flapped them twice, and rose.

As Chine flew into the brightness in the sky, Alex saw a green flash, and everything disappeared.

Alex woke up, gasping for air. All of Boundless surrounded her, Chine's wings over them all. Jim grabbed Alex and held her tightly. "Oh, my God, we didn't think you were going to make it!"

He helped Alex to her feet while Chine pulled his wings back to give Alex space to move. "What happened?"

The dragonriders looked at each other. "We don't know," Gill said. "We saw the flame vortex. In space. That shouldn't be possible. It must have been magic, or something else. But whatever it was, once the flames died, we came through. Both you and Chine were covered in black fire. Chine's breathing apparatus was broken, and we assumed yours was too. You were both unconscious. Then his came back online, and you woke up."

Gill handed Alex her dragon anchor, and she slipped it back on. An alert said she was at a dangerous level of draconic fluid. "I-I think I used the draconic fluid without the anchor. Straight from Chine."

"Maybe that was enough to jump-start the whole system. But who cares how it worked? You're alive."

As the dragonriders crowded around Alex, she saw Vardis walking toward them. He held a red rod in his hand, not very different from the black rods that had been used to disable the dragonrider's anchors earlier. "So, you got your weapon?"

Vardis held it up for everyone to see. "Yes. We do."

Alex reached out. "Give it to me so we can get going."

Vardis halted, looking from the stone to Alex. "What do you mean?"

"Boundless was tasked with getting this. You were supposed to lead us to it. We're the ones transporting it for safekeeping, so it should be with me, right?"

Vardis handed the rod to Alex. "That seems right."

Alex took the weapon and her anchor absorbed it. She looked around the moon's surface. "Let's go. I've had enough of the moon for a lifetime."

No one from Boundless disagreed, but Alex could see Vardis was still watching her as if he expected her to give the rod back. She didn't, instead leaping onto Chine and rising into the sky.

Boundless swooped around the moon and headed for Earth. Alex wasn't sure what the hell was going on, but she knew Myrddin needed the rod as soon as possible. He also had to hear what had happened.

Jim's voice came over the comm. "Okay, guys, we have a real big problem. Incoming bogies—"

Before he could finish speaking, a portal opened a few thousand miles from Boundless. Vrosks and harpies flew out, followed by a black cloud that distorted space around it.

A deep voice screeched through Alex's mind. Judging by the scream of her teammates over the comm, they all heard it as well.

"Alex Bound, you heard what my master said. Will you help me destroy the weapon, or will I have to kill you to keep it from destroying all of reality?"

There was silence as creatures poured out of the open portal.

Alex stared at the sheer number of creatures coming through the portal, at the mass of tendrils and tentacles stretching out. Something like a ship that seemed to be more flesh than machine was making its way through.

The portal grew, stretching to accommodate the living ship, a cylinder covered in all things that creep and crawl through the worst dreams humans could create. It was from a place beyond madness, and the voice was coming from it.

Alex stared into the blackness of space, quickly filling with dark creatures, and watched the tendrils of the Dark One extending toward her.

"I have come for you, Alex," he said.

Alex could barely hear his voice over Boundless' screams. The movies were wrong. You *could* hear screams in space.

Sometimes your worst enemy is also the voice of reason. And when the Dark One shows Alex something unexpected, Alex is forced to wonder if the Dark One is telling the truth or not. Because if he is telling the truth, then all live everywhere is at risk of annihilation.

AUTHOR NOTES RAMY VANCE

MAY 2, 2020

It finally happened. Dragons in space!

And that's how this whole thing started to begin with. Michael had asked me what I wanted to write about and the first thought that came to mind was: Dragons in space.

Damn… I just love saying that: Dragons in space. It doesn't get old. And seeing the wide image of this just blows me away. Jake Caleb – the cover designer for ALL the Middang3ard books – really broke the mold with this one.

As soon as lockdown is over (we're in the throes of Covid-19 for those of you reading this down the line), I'm going to print shop and turning this into a poster for my wall!

Which brings me to my next point – would you also like a high-rez image to make your own poster? Well here you go, loyal fans!

CLICK HERE to get the image

You don't have to do this, but we'd really appreciate if you helped us get the word out about the series. Post the image on Facebook, Twitter, Instagram – you're local community board. Add #DragonsinSpace on the post and a link to Book 1 in the series. You'd be doing us – and Team Boundless – a solid!

Thank you!

And thank you, Michael Anderle! We did it. 10 months and 9 novellas later, we did it!

Dragons in friggin' space!

AUTHOR NOTES MICHAEL ANDERLE

MAY 3, 2020

THANK YOU for reading our story!

We have a few of these planned, but we don't know if we should continue writing and publishing without your input.

Options include leaving a review, reaching out on Facebook to let us know, and smoke signals.

Frankly, smoke signals might get misconstrued as low hanging clouds, so you might want to nix that idea...

And that's how this whole thing started.

Ramy's author notes: "Michael had asked me what I wanted to write about, and the first thought that came to mind was: dragons in space."

Now, dragons in space are cool. Dragons are cool. You could put dragons in the frozen tundra, and I'm going to think "cool."

But, Dragons in 'xxx' is like peanut butter and chocolate. Unfortunately, Ramy tried his next idea on me, which was "Samurai vs. Vampires." I had to say no. He continued to pepper me with efforts to persuade me. I said no again.

I might have said, "Hell, no."

Instead of trying to push the effort, I think he implemented a guerrilla warfare tactic and started peppering my virtual office with sexy gnome concepts. He even put my video images to Amazon sexy gnome products.

I finally figured out his deviant plan. He is trying to get me to be so disgusted with his next few ideas that samurai and vampires seem plausible in comparison.

Sorry, Ramy, the answer (for anything gnome) and the Samurai / Vampire options are a hard...

No.

Keep trying, Mr. Vance.

Ad Aeternitatem,

Michael Anderle

OTHER BOOKS BY THE AUTHORS

Other Middang3ard Books

Never Split The Party (01)
Late To the Party (02)
It's My Party (03)
Blue Hell And Alien Fire (04)

Death Of An Author: A Middang3ard Novella

Other Books by Ramy Vance

Mortality Bites Series
Keep Evolving Series
Fatebound Series
Welcome to the Dragon Show Series

Other Books by Michael Anderle

For a complete list of books by Michael Anderle, please visit:

www.lmbpn.com/ma-books/

All LMBPN Audiobooks are Available at Audible.com and
iTunes. To see all LMBPN audiobooks, including those
written by Michael Anderle please visit:

www.lmbpn.com/audible

CONNECT WITH THE AUTHORS

Connect with Ramy

Join Ramy's Newsletter to get a **FREE AUDIOBOOK!**
Join Ramy's FB Group: House of the GoneGod Damned!

Connect with Michael Anderle and sign up for his email list here:

Website: http://lmbpn.com

Email List: http://lmbpn.com/email/

Facebook:
www.facebook.com/TheKurtherianGambitBooks